WOBBLEBOTTOM

MOST WANTED

D.R. FOSTER

DEDICATION

TABLE OF CONTENTS

Chapter 1
Trouble Brews
in Wobblealot

It was an unusually peaceful morning in the Kingdom of Wobblealot.

The sun rose like a slightly confused pancake, wobbling on the horizon. Birds chirped, villagers bustled, and somewhere nearby, Sir Wobblebottom, the Kingdom's most unlikely hero, let out a heroic snore followed by a trumpet-like fart that rattled the castle windows.

King Arthur of Wobblealot, currently halfway through his morning tea, sighed into his cup. "Every day," he muttered, wiping condensation off the glass, "it's like living inside a brass band made entirely of hippo."

Sir Wobblebottom, the five-tonne, gloriously pink hippopotamus-knight, lay sprawled across the Royal Stable Courtyard, snoring like a broken tuba. His ceremonial knighthood sash was wrapped around one leg, his golden crown sat askew over one ear, and someone had tied a sign to his tail that read:

"DO NOT DISTURB (Unless to Feed Watermelon Rinds)."

It had been weeks since the infamous Quest for the Golden Gravy Boat. Since then, Wobblebottom's legend had only grown. Songs were sung. Flags were waved. Small children traded collectible Wobblebottom trading cards. He was, as the local bard put it, "the pride of Wobblealot and the bane of unsuspecting nostrils everywhere."

Not that Sir Wobblebottom noticed. He spent most days snacking on watermelon rinds, flattening garden gnomes, and—according to increasingly frustrated royal gardeners—accidentally moonwalking through flowerbeds.

"Have you seen the posters?" came a panicked voice from down the hall.

It was Kevin, the royal stable boy, bursting into the throne room, looking pale, breathless, and wildly alarmed. This wasn't unusual. Kevin was frightened of loud noises, unexpected shadows, and—according to castle gossip—his own reflection on particularly shiny floors.

He was also holding a crumpled scroll in one trembling hand, and his tunic appeared to be inside out.

"What posters?" Arthur asked, lowering his tea and eyeing the mop Kevin had clearly dragged in with him.

Kevin held up the parchment. In bold, oily lettering, it read:

"WANTED: THE LEGENDARY PINK HIPPO OF WOBBLEALOT — DEAD OR ALIVE

(Preferably Alive, Payback Required... but Dead Works Too)"

Underneath was a dramatically overflattering artistic interpretation of Sir Wobblebottom, looking far more majestic and significantly slimmer than reality. He even had visible abs.

"Where did you get this?" Arthur demanded, snatching it.

"They're everywhere! The tavern walls, the market stalls—even the royal bakery had one jammed in the scone display!" Kevin panted. "Somebody's put a bounty on Sir Wobblebottom!"

Arthur's eyes narrowed. "Who would dare target my royal steed?"

Before Kevin could answer, a commotion erupted from the courtyard.

The sound of startled chickens, clanging buckets, and someone yelling, 'I've lost my trousers!' drifted through the stained-glass windows.

They rushed to the nearest window—just in time to see a group of shadowy, hooded figures attempting to roll, lasso, and generally wrangle a confused but still snoring Sir Wobblebottom onto a very large, rickety wagon.

Wobblebottom snorted in his sleep, rolled over, and blasted a heroic fart that sent the kidnappers into total disarray. One dropped the rope and ran in circles holding his nose. Another dove headfirst into a hedge. A third simply froze, eyes watering, whispering, "I wasn't trained for this..."

"Oh no," Arthur groaned. "They're actually doing it."

"We have to stop them!" Kevin cried, already hyperventilating. "They've got ropes! And wheels! And—oh no—is that a vat of barbecue sauce?!"

It was.

But it was too late. With surprising efficiency—and after at least three of the kidnappers were accidentally sat on—the mysterious figures managed to haul Wobblebottom up a wooden ramp, tie him down with vines, and rumble off down the castle road at top speed. One of them was waving a flag that read:

"WE DID A THING!"

"What thing?" muttered a nearby goose, but nobody heard her.

A note was nailed to the castle gate, with a custard tart.

Arthur peeled it off gingerly and read aloud:

"To the so-called 'heroes' of Wobblealot:

The pink menace is ours. At last, justice (and possibly vengeance, and definitely dramatic payback) shall be served.

He humiliated me in Grizzleham. He bellyflopped upon my empire, crushed my dreams, and flattened my dignity into the gravy-soaked dirt.

Now I shall reclaim my honour one ridiculous hoof at a time.

Signed,

LORD LARDINGTON

(Supreme Overlord of the Land of Lard, Conqueror of Condiments, Master of Slightly Too Much Eyeliner)"

Arthur blinked. "Someone's been holding a grudge... and possibly a thesaurus."

Out in the courtyard, the trail of destruction left behind was... oddly lumpy. Deep boot prints. Shattered barrels. A faint smell of stew. Arthur frowned. "Those weren't ordinary bandits..."

As the wagon disappeared into the distance, bouncing over cabbages and knocking over a pastry cart, the Kingdom of Wobblealot erupted into chaos. Peasants screamed. Horses neighed. Someone fainted into a wheelbarrow of leeks.

"Send word to Baron Twitchwhiskers!" Arthur bellowed. "We need—"

"Already here," came a dramatically small voice from the bookshelf.

Baron Twitchwhiskers, aristocratic squirrel of mystery and drama, had apparently been listening from a teacup behind the throne. His monocle gleamed. His cape was freshly pressed. His tiny cravat fluttered in the breeze from a nearby fan.

"We must rescue Sir Wobblebottom," Arthur declared.

"Yes," Twitchwhiskers agreed, hopping down with flair. "But I am not leaving this castle. It has central heating.

Heated seats. And a cheese cellar with twelve varieties of brie. We shall orchestrate his rescue... remotely."

Arthur rubbed his temples. "It's going to be one of those quests, isn't it?"

Sir Wobblebottom snored—somewhere in the distance—completely unaware that his most ridiculous, most perilous, and most flatulence-filled adventure was only just beginning.

Chapter 2
Operation
Hippo Retrieval

Castle Wobblealot was in chaos. Servants ran in every direction, shouting. A knight fainted into a fruit basket. Somewhere, a bard was composing a tragic ballad far too soon.

King Arthur stood in the Great Hall, hair sticking out at strange angles, eyes wild. His royal bathrobe trailed behind him like a defeated flag.

"He's gone!" Arthur cried, pacing wildly. "They've taken him! Sir Wobblebottom! The bravest, stinkiest, most majestic creature this kingdom has ever seen!"

"Technically, the only creature weighing more than a small cottage," Baron Twitchwhiskers muttered from his velvet throne by the fire, lazily spooning marmalade onto a croissant.

Arthur ignored him, turning to the panicking crowd. "We have to mount a rescue! Search the woods! Mobilise the knights! Someone alert the Cheese Guild; they always know things!"

Twitchwhiskers adjusted his monocle. "If trolls are involved, of course, Lardington's pulling the strings. Trolls don't plan. They bicker, they nap, and occasionally they sit on things by accident. They'd never have managed this without a moustache-twirling maniac yelling at them."

Across the hall, Kevin, the stable boy, was trying very hard to melt into the curtains. He shook with terror, clutching a mop as though it might fend off an army. His eyes darted toward the stables outside, wide with fear.

"You!" Arthur pointed dramatically at Kevin.

Kevin squeaked. "Me? No—no, I'm just the stable boy. I clean... stable things. And mop things. I—I don't do heroic things."

"You know Sir Wobblebottom best," Arthur declared. "You handle his... erm... dietary mishaps. You can track him!"

Kevin stuttered. "No, no, no, Your Majesty, I—I can't possibly. I'm terrible with... with... with missing hippos! And—and..." He lowered his voice, glancing nervously toward the empty stables. "Horses."

Arthur frowned. "There aren't any horses here."

"Yet," Kevin whispered darkly.

Baron Twitchwhiskers rolled his eyes. "The king's prized steed, Sir Lancealot, is still off at Jousting School, Kevin. You're safe from hoof-related trauma, at least."

Kevin shivered. "Safe? Last year, every time that horse ran off, I had to chase him down! He cornered me in a fruit cart once. I still flinch when I smell pineapples!"

Arthur sighed. "No horses. Just woods. Possibly bandits. Maybe some mushroom-related injuries."

Kevin whimpered again. "I don't do adventures!" and then quickly added, "Or kidnappings! Or—or squirrels with swords!"

Baron Twitchwhiskers waved a paw. "Relax, boy. You won't be alone."

Arthur scowled. "Wait... you're coming with us?"

The squirrel scoffed. "Absolutely not. I have discovered something remarkable since our last quest."

Arthur raised an eyebrow. "Which is?"

"Indoor plumbing," Twitchwhiskers declared, gesturing grandly to the castle. Heated floors. Pillows with actual stuffing. I nearly died last time, and I have no intention of sleeping in the dirt again."

He began ticking items off on his paw. "I've also discovered: a bubble bath with honey infusion, biscuits that arrive on silver trays, and a mysterious device in the pantry that toasts crumpets on both sides. I will not be leaving all that behind to traipse through the mud like some common adventurer with twigs in their trousers."

Arthur spluttered. "But... but Wobblebottom—

"Deserves a rescue," Twitchwhiskers interrupted. "And he shall have one. But I will coordinate this daring operation from right here, where the tea is hot and the chairs don't have twigs in them."

Kevin's eyes darted between them. "So... I have to go out there? By myself? With... bandits? And monsters? And whatever took Sir Wobblebottom? And probably... horses?"

"Don't be ridiculous," Twitchwhiskers said. "Arthur's going with you."

Arthur's jaw dropped. "I'm the king!"

"And I'm the strategic genius who isn't risking mud on his fur," Twitchwhiskers replied smoothly. "Face it, Arthur. The people need you. The hippo needs you. Kevin needs— well, several things—but courage is top of the list."

Kevin whimpered.

"Perhaps we send... someone else?" Kevin offered weakly. "Sir Blunderhelm? He's got a sword. Or—or that butler with the scary eyebrows. Or maybe we train some very brave squirrels? I can help from here. Very helpful. Excellent curtain hiding."

Arthur raised an eyebrow.

"Fine," Kevin said quickly, eyes darting. "Then maybe... I'm not Kevin. I'm... Devin. A different stable boy. Kevin left. Said something about moving to a nice, quiet swamp." Twitchwhiskers didn't even look up. "Nice try, Kevin."

Kevin deflated.

Twitchwhiskers unrolled a map across the table, pointing with his tiny paw. "I've already had reports.

Wobblebottom was last seen being hauled onto a cart of questionable structural integrity, heading toward the Whispering Woods."

"The Whispering Woods?" Arthur groaned. "They whisper ominous things! And the mushrooms bite!"

"Precisely why I'm staying here," Twitchwhiskers said cheerfully, tossing Kevin a small crystal. "This is a scrying stone. I'll watch your every move. Offer advice. Possibly criticism."

Arthur sighed, rubbing his temples. "We're doomed."

"We'll get him back," Twitchwhiskers promised, already settling deeper into his chair. "Or you will, with my impeccable guidance."

Outside, distant thunder rumbled ominously. Kevin made a small whimpering noise, clutched his mop tighter, and tried not to picture Gallopadonk—the terrifying carnival pony who once chased him through a hedge maze.

The rescue mission had begun—whether they liked it or not.

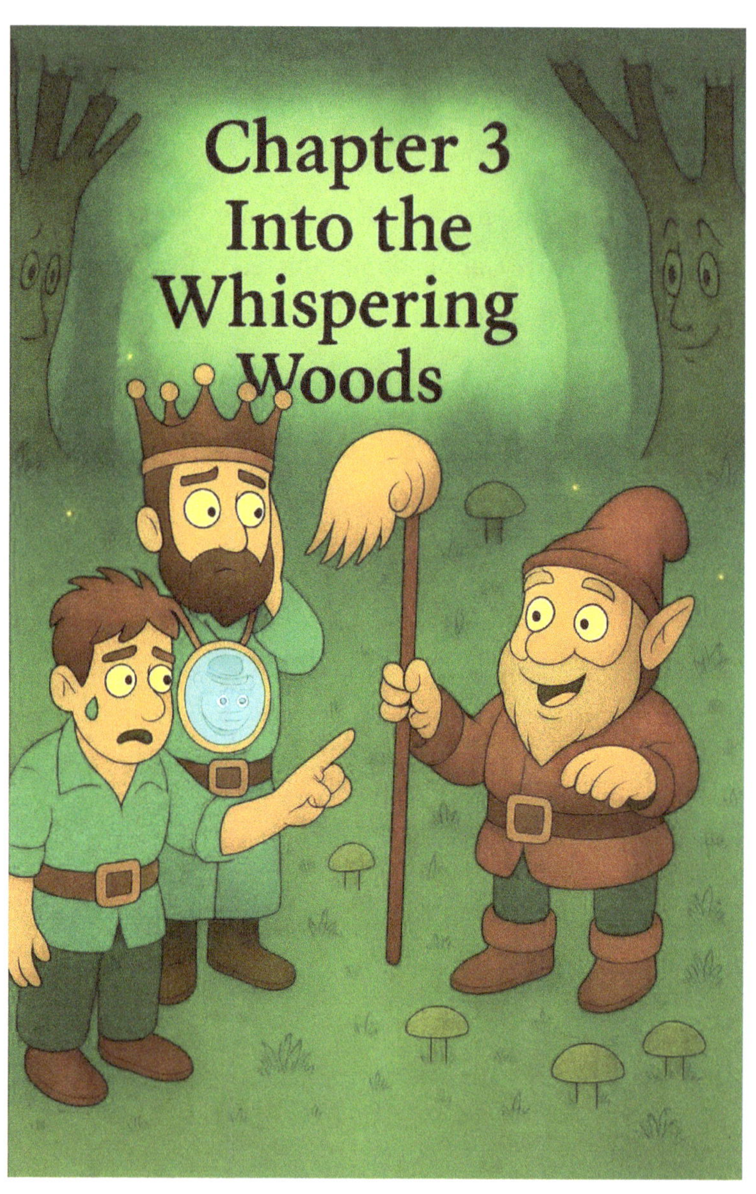

Chapter 3
Into the
Whispering
Woods

The Whispering Woods loomed ahead, dark, tangled, and entirely too atmospheric for Kevin's liking. The trees bent and twisted unnaturally, their gnarled branches forming claw-like arches over the narrow trail. Faint voices drifted on the wind—half warnings, half gossip.

"They forgot the gravy..."

"Turn back, turn back... or bring snacks."

"The boy smells like fear and cabbage."

"This is a terrible idea," Kevin whimpered, gripping his mop with white knuckles.

King Arthur, dressed in ill-fitting travel gear and an expression of deep regret, led the way. "It's not ideal," the king admitted. "But Wobblebottom's out there. Somewhere."

Behind them, Baron Twitchwhiskers' voice crackled through the enchanted scrying stone dangling around Arthur's neck.

"Turn left at the creepy rock formation that looks like an angry badger," the squirrel's voice instructed. "Avoid the mushrooms. They bite."

Arthur sighed. "Must be nice, offering advice from your heated chair while we wrestle with whispering bushes."

"I'm strategically comfortable," Twitchwhiskers replied smugly.

The trail narrowed, roots coiling across the path like tripwires. Strange plants blinked as they passed. One tree chuckled softly. Kevin let out a yelp.

"Did that bush just giggle at me?" he hissed.

Arthur didn't answer. He was too busy swatting away a vine that had tried to braid his hair.

A sudden rustle in the bushes sent Kevin into a frenzy. He shrieked, clutching his mop like a sword, jabbing wildly at the undergrowth. "Back! Back, I say! I have cleaning supplies and no sense of restraint!"

Arthur paused, frowning. "Kevin… why in the name of Wobblealot did you bring a mop?"

"It's—it's what I know!" Kevin stammered, holding the mop tighter. "It's sturdy! Reliable! Cleans up after… well, incidents!"

Arthur raised an eyebrow. "You're marching into the most dangerous forest in the kingdom armed with a glorified sponge on a stick?"

Kevin's lower lip quivered. "Swords are sharp! They're pointy! I could trip and… impale myself. Or someone else! The mop is… much less lethal."

Arthur sighed, rubbing his temples. "Remind me never to put you in charge of battle strategy."

"Technically," Kevin muttered, "this is a rescue mission. There will probably be… messes."

Before Arthur could retort, the bushes exploded with movement. Out tumbled a small, disgruntled gnome— acorn slingshot in hand, eyes narrowed.

"You there!" the gnome barked, glaring at them. "Trespassers! This is sacred, whispering land!"

"We're just—" Arthur began.

"Kidnappers?" the gnome interrupted.

"No!" Kevin squeaked. "Victims of... of... circumstantial adventuring!"

The gnome frowned. "Hmph. You've got the look of mushroom-stompers about you."

"We're looking for a..." Arthur hesitated, glancing at Kevin, "a five-tonne pink hippo." The gnome's expression didn't change.

"Knighted," Arthur added quickly. "Royal steed. Extremely flatulent. You'd remember him."

The gnome's eyes widened slightly. "Oh... him."

Kevin perked up. "You've seen Sir Wobblebottom?"

"Might have," the gnome replied, twirling his slingshot. "But nothing's free in the Whispering Woods."

Arthur groaned. "What do you want? Gold? Favors? Cryptic riddles?"

The gnome pointed at Kevin's mop. "That."

Kevin's mouth fell open in horror. "My... mop?"

"Best weapon I've seen all week," the gnome said, nodding appreciatively.

"Can't we offer you something else?" Arthur asked. "That mop is the only thing keeping him from full-blown panic screaming."

"I want the mop."

Kevin clutched it to his chest. "We've been through so much together. Stables, Porridge spills. The time Sir Wobblebottom got stuck in the fountain and panicked."

Arthur clapped Kevin on the shoulder. "Congratulations, you're finally useful."

Kevin whimpered as he reluctantly handed over the mop.

The gnome grinned, tucking it under his arm like a prized sword. "Your hippo was taken toward the northern glen. Strange folk—big cart. Bad wheels."

Arthur straightened. "Thank you."

The gnome saluted with the mop, then vanished into the undergrowth, leaving only the faint sound of humming and one very confused mushroom.

Kevin sagged with despair. "We're doomed."

"Nonsense," Arthur declared, squaring his shoulders. "We've got determination, directions, and—"

"No weapon," Kevin pointed out.

"Small details," Arthur muttered.

Kevin knelt beside a stick, tied a soggy leaf to it with a shoelace, and held it up like a sword.

"Sir Mopsalot would've wanted me to carry on," he said solemnly.

Over the scrying stone, Twitchwhiskers' voice crackled with amusement.

"Splendid progress, gentlemen. You've traded your only weapon for directions... and a gnome is now armed with cleaning supplies."

Arthur groaned. "This mission... is off to a fantastic start."

Chapter 4
Trouble in the Trolling Grounds

The map was glowing again.

Not in the traditional magical way—no elegant scrolls or glittery runes here. This one pulsed gently with a trail of neon green slime that spelled out **YOU ARE (PROBABLY) HERE** and pointed vaguely northeast.

A passing firefly blinked LOL in Morse code before flying into a tree.

"I'm not convinced this map knows what it's doing," King Arthur muttered, holding it at arm's length.

Kevin trudged behind him, clutching his empty hands miserably. "I miss my mop."

"You gave it away," Arthur said flatly.

"You made me!" Kevin countered. "Actually, you demanded it."

"Gentlemen," Baron Twitchwhiskers' voice crackled through the scrying stone at Arthur's neck, "if you're quite finished bickering about poor life choices, you're nearly at the Trolling Grounds."

They emerged from the trees and stopped.

The Trolling Grounds stretched out before them—wide, rocky, and utterly unwelcoming.

Mossy boulders hunched together like gossiping old women.

Makeshift rope bridges sagged between jagged rocks.

Caves burped steam for no visible reason.

The air was thick with the scent of damp moss and something that might have been stew, or possibly regret.

Faint bellowing echoed in the distance—followed by someone shouting, **"I SAID NO SPOILERS, DAVE!"**

Kevin whimpered. "This place feels like it wants to give me nightmares... and then slow clap when they come true."

"Keep moving," Arthur said. "The sooner we find Wobblebottom, the sooner we can leave."

They followed the glowing slime trail through a twisting gorge where the rocks glistened suspiciously.

Strange squelching sounds rose from cracks.

A troll-sized footprint squelched audibly as Kevin accidentally stepped in it.

"This is the worst path I've ever taken," Kevin whispered.

"You've only taken one path," Arthur replied.

"Exactly."

Just ahead, the ground opened into a wide, shallow pit.

Dozens of trolls lounged around in various states of discontent.

Some sat on rocks muttering complaints about soup temperatures.

Others waved signs reading **DOWN WITH GRAVEL** and **BRING BACK SWAMP TUESDAYS.**

One troll sat under a dripping stalactite, looking personally betrayed by gravity.

Arthur swallowed hard. "All right. Let's stay calm. There are too many. We can't fight our way through."

"Fight?" Kevin squeaked. "I was planning on fainting and hoping they would politely ignore me!"

"Quiet," Arthur hissed. "Stay low. We'll circle around."

They crept along the ridge, hearts hammering. Kevin nearly sneezed on a glow beetle. One troll sniffed the air, and Arthur yanked Kevin flat behind a mossy log just in time.

When the bellowing finally faded behind them, Kevin sagged against a tree. "I can't feel my everything."

"Keep moving," Arthur muttered. "Before one of them decides we look snack-sized."

They pushed deeper into the gorge, and that's when a nearby rock stood up, sniffed the air, and blinked.

"Oi," said the rock.

Kevin screamed.

The rock brushed moss out of its eyebrows.

It was very clearly a troll wearing a name tag that read: **HELLO, MY NAME IS CHONK.**

"You two look like quest types," Chonk said gruffly. "We don't like quest types."

"We're just… passing through," Arthur said carefully. "On an extremely low-stakes, non-epic sort of journey."

Chonk snorted. "Right. You're holding a glowing map and talking to a magical rock necklace. Totally casual."

"I told you the map was too loud," Kevin hissed.

Chonk planted his enormous hands on his knees. "Toll time. You want to cross Troll Land, you gotta answer a riddle."

Arthur straightened. "Riddles I can do."

Chonk unrolled a scroll. "What is big, pink, round, and currently very much kidnapped?"

Arthur's mouth opened, then closed. "That's not a riddle, that's… news."

"TROLL RIDDLE," Chonk barked.

Kevin squeaked, "Sir Wobblebottom?"

"Correct," Chonk nodded. "You may proceed. But you didn't hear it from me—he's being held up north, in the Cliffs of Grumbles.

Did they ask me to help drag him there? Nooo. Said I was 'too dainty for heavy lifting.'" He folded his arms. "So fine. Let them strain their spines."

Arthur blinked. "The Cliffs of Grumbles?"

"Yep." Chonk lowered his voice conspiratorially. "Used to be trolls only kidnapped goats. Now they take orders from that greasy suit-wearer... Lardington.

Said the pink one, bellyflopped on his gravy empire and flattened his ego like a soggy flapjack."

Kevin's eyes went wide.

Chonk rubbed his forehead. "Honestly, the whole camp's a disaster. Half of them are trying to build a roasting spit they're not even allowed to use; the other half are arguing about whether he's a magical pudding or a war beast. Someone even claimed his farts might count as seasoning."

He snorted. "They know they can't actually eat him—Lardington wants him alive for his big revenge show. But trolls love to argue about meals they'll never get to eat."

Arthur's stomach twisted. "Eat? They want to eat him?!"

"Want to, yes. Allowed to, absolutely not," Chonk said. "One bite and Lardington will turn them into troll jerky."

Kevin made a strangled noise. "They're going to pudding the hippo?!"

"Relax," said Chonk. "They'll be arguing for hours before anyone thinks about chewing. You've got time."

Arthur glanced at the glowing slime trail, then back to Chonk. "Thank you."

"Don't thank me," Chonk said. "I never said this conversation happened."

He handed them a sagging paper bag. "Cheese rinds. For luck."

Then he gave Kevin a cracked kazoo. "For emergencies. Or, you know ...pretending you've got friends." Chonk threw back his head and let out a booming laugh that echoed off the rocks. Kevin flinched like it might knock him over.

Kevin held the cracked kazoo like it might explode. "We're doomed."

"Nonsense," Arthur said, squaring his shoulders. "We've got directions, supplies, and—"

"Seventeen new smells haunting my nightmares," Kevin muttered.

"Positivity, Kevin," Arthur muttered.

Far behind them, the troll voices had already faded back into arguments about soup. Chonk watched them leave with a shrug, then plodded off in the opposite direction, muttering about how underappreciated his boulder-lifting skills were.

"Excellent work," came Baron Twitchwhiskers' overly cheerful voice. "Judging by the trail, your next destination is the Cliffs of Grumbles. Very ominous. Very dramatic. Perfectly suited for a heroic song involving screaming, splatting, and possibly kazoo solos."

Kevin whimpered. "Brilliant. I can trip over flat ground—now you want me near cliffs?"

Arthur muttered, "Marvelous. Now the cliffs won't be the only things grumbling."

Kevin sighed and tucked the kazoo into his belt like a tiny, very disappointing sword. Glowing slime clung to their boots as they trudged onward—toward the Cliffs of Grumbles, and whatever ridiculous nonsense waited with their missing hippo.

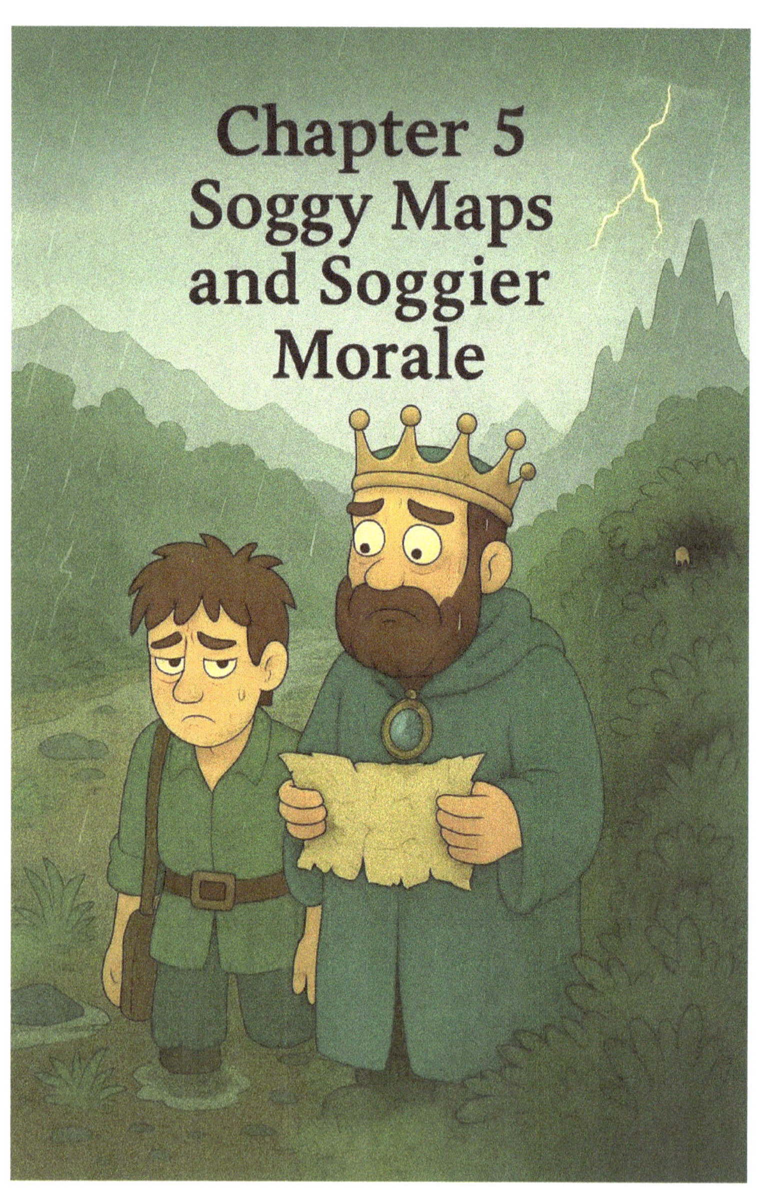

Chapter 5
Soggy Maps
and Soggier
Morale

The rain began somewhere between the Trolling Grounds and the Cliffs of Grumbles, and it hadn't stopped since.

Kevin trudged behind King Arthur, soaked to the knees and clutching the remains of what had once been a respectable snack satchel. Now it was just cheese mush and experiential dread.

Arthur, for his part, was looking increasingly like a disgruntled laundry pile in boots. His once-noble cloak stuck to him like a wet leaf. The enchanted scrying stone dangled around his neck, glowing faintly and humming what might have been a passive-aggressive lullaby.

"I can't feel my toes," Kevin moaned.

"You're lucky," Arthur grumbled. "I'm fairly sure mine have mutinied."

"Do we even know where we're going?"

Arthur pulled out the soggy map and squinted. The once-glowing trail was now mostly smeared neon slime and one shifty-looking mushroom stain.

"Well," he said slowly, "I think we're near the Ridge of Reasonably Large Rodents. Or possibly the Gorge of Goblins with Poor Hygiene. Hard to tell—everything's gone a bit... melty."

Behind them, a bush sneezed.

Kevin yelped and leapt behind a tree. "We're being followed!"

Arthur peered at the bush. "No. That's just the wind. Or the mushroom. Or the wind sneezing through a mushroom. Either way, it's not attacking."

Kevin peeked out. "Are you sure?"

Arthur sighed. "If I responded to every suspicious bush in these woods, I'd have declared war on an entire hedge last week."

The scrying stone buzzed. Baron Twitchwhiskers' voice crackled through, clear and far too chipper.

"Ah! There you are. Still alive, I see. Delightful."

Arthur groaned. "Twitchwhiskers, if you say 'I told you so' again, I'm chucking this rock into a pond."

"Touchy," Twitchwiskers replied. "I was only going to mention that you've veered slightly off course. You're about two hills and a moderately cursed meadow south of where the cart was last spotted."

Kevin squinted at the stone. "Is that... clinking? Are you having tea?"

"Of course I am," Twitchwhiskers said. "Also, scones. And a very agreeable cheese board. It's important to keep one's strength up during an operation of this scale."

Arthur's eye twitched. "You're still in the castle."

"Obviously. The bathwater is the perfect temperature, the chairs have actual cushioning, and someone just brought me a hot towel that smells faintly of cinnamon. Why in Wobblealot would I be out there getting rained on?"

Kevin made a strangled sound. "We're freezing. And damp. And possibly moulding."

"That's the spirit," Twitchwhiskers said breezily. "Anyway, do hurry up.

Wobblebottom isn't going to rescue himself."

"Hurry up?" Kevin hissed. "We're lost?"

"Not lost," Twitchwhiskers said. "Just... strategically rerouted."

Arthur wiped slime off his sleeve. "Can you just point us in the right direction?"

"Head northeast until you hear the sound of yodeling frogs. You'll pass the Boiling Puddle of Mild Inconvenience, then cross over the Log of Eternal Wobble. You'll be back on track in no time."

Kevin blinked. "That can't be a real log."

"It is. And it's very wobbly," Twitchwhiskers confirmed.

They marched on in silence, interrupted only by Kevin slipping on a particularly rude-looking root and Arthur fighting off a mildly flirtatious vine.

By nightfall, they'd made it to a sheltered hollow beneath an overhanging ledge shaped suspiciously like a disapproving librarian.

Kevin flopped onto a pile of leaves. "Do you think Wobblebottom's okay?"

Arthur leaned against a rock, staring up at the sky. "I don't know. But I do know one thing."

"What?"

Arthur closed his eyes. "If the first thing he does is fart on me… I'm un-knighting him."

Kevin rummaged through his satchel, hunting for something that hadn't dissolved into mush. A lump of damp cheese and a biscuit that looked like it had already been eaten once were all that stared back at him. He sighed and picked at it, rain dripping from his nose. "Typical," he muttered. "Twitchwhiskers gets tea and scones while I get mould in a bag. He's the one with the brains, the maps, the vocabulary; he should be out here! What did I do wrong? Feed the wrong horse? Mop the wrong floor? This feels like punishment for something I don't even remember doing."

Arthur said nothing. He simply leaned back against the rock, rain sliding through his hair, letting Kevin's grumbling fade into the steady rhythm of the storm. For a long moment, neither of them spoke. The hollow filled with the sound of rain and the occasional grumble of thunder, and somewhere nearby, a frog croaked like it was laughing at them.

A hush settled over the hollow — until the wind delivered a faint, familiar PFFFFFT.

Kevin sat bolt upright. "Did you hear that?"

Arthur's eyes widened. "That was—!"

"Sir Wobblebottom!" they shouted in unison.

Hope surged. Wobblebottom was near; the smell proved it.

Chapter 6
The Trail
of the Toot

They ran.

Well—Arthur ran. Kevin stumbled, tripped over a log, got tangled in a fern, and then ran, clutching a broken twig like it might protect him from hippo-stealing trolls.

"The sound came from that direction!" Arthur shouted, pointing toward a shadowy ravine lined with weeping willow trees that looked like they'd seen too much.

Kevin caught up, wheezing. "What if it was just... a wild wind? Or an especially opinionated duck?"

Arthur frowned. "That was no duck. I'd know that sound anywhere. It was Wobblebottom."

The scrying stone around Arthur's neck buzzed. Baron Twitchwhiskers' voice piped in, slightly muffled by what sounded suspiciously like biscuit crumbs.

"Ah, yes, the Noble Flatulence Locator System. Primitive, yet oddly effective. I've recalibrated the scrying stone to trace residual air displacement patterns. You're on the right track—though I do suggest holding your breath."

Kevin gagged. "You can track farts?"

"Great heroes track what they must," Twitchwhiskers replied, and then added, "Also, I may have scented the castle air with lavender to counteract the memory. It's delightful in here."

Arthur growled. "We are trudging through mud, and you are doing interior design."

"Oh, and having cocoa," Twitchwhiskers said breezily. "With whipped cream. One must maintain morale."

The trail was unmistakable now. Branches were broken. Ferns were flattened. The occasional stunned woodland creature blinked at them in silent, wide-eyed horror.

And then they reached it.

The Cart.

Or what remained of it.

A massive wooden wagon lay toppled on its side in a clearing. One wheel had splintered entirely, and deep hippo-shaped drag marks continued into the forest beyond.

Kevin crept forward, nose wrinkling. "It smells like…
sweaty trolls and flatulence."

Arthur nodded grimly. "Definitely Wobblebottom."

Around the wreckage lay all manner of odd debris:
cracked jars of what appeared to be gravy confetti, a
crushed trumpet, half a "World's Best Villain" mug, and a
pile of abandoned troll snack wrappers labelled
Explosive Onion Crisps – Do Not Ignite.

Kevin stared. "This looks like… like chaos in snack form."

"Then we are close," Arthur said darkly.

A shredded banner hung from the cart's edge. It read, in bold, oily letters:

**PROPERTY OF THE LAND OF LARD –
MUSTACHES ARE MANDATORY.**

Arthur's stomach sank. "Lardington."

Twitchwhiskers' voice crackled again. "Told you he'd resurface. Honestly, we should've stuffed him in a barrel after last time. A small barrel. With air holes, obviously."

Kevin squeaked. "Mandatory moustaches? What if you can't grow one? Do they... glue it on you?!"

Arthur pinched the bridge of his nose. "It's not always about you, Kevin."

Kevin shrank back, fiddling with the cracked kazoo. "So... who is this Lardington, then? And why does his name sound like a greasy side dish?"

Arthur's jaw clenched. "He's the villainous beanpole with an outrageously enormous moustache who tried to flood Grizzleham with gravy. We defeated him—barely. Now he's back. And he's taken Wobblebottom."

Kevin looked pale. "Why would anyone kidnap a flatulent hippo?"

Arthur sighed. "Because he's brave. Because he's royal. Because he once saved an entire village using nothing but his left cheek and a strong breeze. And because he ended Lardington's grand gravy-flooding scheme by bellyflopping on him mid-parade—in front of the whole of Grizzleham— and squashed his moustache, his ego, and his big dramatic evil speech all at once."

Twitchwhiskers added, "Frankly, Lardington's pride is still drying out."

Kevin's voice rose in pitch. "What if they... humiliate him? Make him polish Lardington's moustache comb? Or force him to sing lullabies to trolls? Or—" his eyes went wide, "oh no... what if they make his farts come out as sparkly heart-shaped bubbles?!"

Arthur gave him a flat look. "Kevin."

"Sorry. Spiral."

Arthur picked up a piece of slime-covered rope. "They're heading northeast. Toward the Marshes of Mirthless Moaning, then up to the Cliffs of Grumbles."

Kevin groaned. "That sounds awful."

"It is," Twitchwhiskers confirmed. "It's like a bog, but whinier. And everything squelches at you with judgment."

"Of course it does," Kevin muttered.

Arthur shook his head. "Either way, we need rest. We'll camp here, then set out at dawn."

Kevin slumped. "Fantastic. Nothing like trying to sleep with troll slime in your shoes."

From somewhere far ahead, carried on the night wind, came another faint, unmistakable PPBBBBBBT.

Arthur's eyes lit up. "He's still out there."

Chapter 7
The Cliffs
of Grumbles

The Cliffs of Grumbles loomed ahead like the world's angriest birthday cake—grey, jagged, and slouching under their own bad attitude. They weren't just cliffs. They were complaining about cliffs.

"Ugh, not more climbers," grumbled one boulder.

"My ledges hurt," moaned another.

A rock nearby muttered, "Hope you packed splints."

Kevin stopped dead. "The rocks are talking."

Arthur squinted up the sheer wall of stone. "Grumbling," he said. "Hence the name."

"Right," Kevin whispered. "Totally fine. Definitely not a vertical doom stack filled with sentient sarcasm."

The scrying stone at Arthur's neck buzzed. Baron Twitchwhiskers' voice came through, irritatingly cheerful.

"Ah, the Cliffs of Grumbles. Prime villain real estate. If you do fall, at least try not to make a noise that echoes for generations."

Arthur groaned. "Any advice that doesn't involve falling?"

"Certainly. Don't." A delicate clink of China. "Also, my crème Brulé just arrived."

Kevin made a noise like a dying accordion. "We're about to scale a wall that actively insults people, and he's having dessert."

The glowing slime trail wound up the cliff like an unwell snake, pulsing faintly as if muttering "probably this way" under its breath.

Arthur tested the first ledge, then began climbing. "Let's get this over with."

Kevin stared up at the dizzying height. "I can't feel my bravery."

"Try using your legs instead," Arthur said.

They clambered up a goat path barely wider than a bootlace. Loose gravel skittered into the abyss. The cliffs grumbled about insurance paperwork.

Halfway up, Arthur's foot slipped. The path crumbled with a crunch.

"GAH!" Arthur flailed, catching himself on a root.

Kevin shrieked, immediately tangling himself in the rope. A moment later, he was dangling upside down, spinning slowly like a terrified wind chime. "I DON'T WANT TO BECOME CLIFF JAM!"

Far below, a cliff muttered, "Amateurs."

Somehow, they staggered onto a ledge halfway up. It was much wider than the rest... and currently occupied.

A dozen trolls lounged around a cauldron, arguing.

"It's soup, not tar."

"Needs more swamp."

"You always say that, Greg!"

Arthur and Kevin flattened themselves behind a boulder. Troll laundry flapped above them like sullen parade flags—huge, patched trousers ballooning in the wind.

Then Kevin's eyes went round. "Arthur... look."

Arthur followed his gaze—and his stomach dropped.

A massive rope lift creaked against the cliff. On it, trussed up like an enormous pink sofa, Sir Wobblebottom was being winched skyward.

His golden crown had slid down over one ear. A vine was tied around his belly like an oversized seatbelt.

He looked vaguely bored, as though this were just an unusually inconvenient nap.

Then the lift jolted—and Wobblebottom let out a muffled **PFFFT** that echoed across the cliffs like distant thunder.

The trolls hauling the ropes winced. The cauldron lid rattled. One troll quietly lay down on the floor and reconsidered life.

"Ah," Twitchwhiskers murmured through the scrying stone. "Still armed and dangerous."

Kevin clutched Arthur's sleeve. "They've got him. They've actually got him."

Arthur's jaw tightened. "Then we get him back."

Kevin hissed, "Oh, brilliant. And how exactly do we politely borrow a kidnapped hippo from a troll fortress?"

"Working on it."

The cliffs grumbled somewhere overhead. Seagulls wheeled above them, shrieking insults.

"Nice boots, cabbage face!" one called.

Kevin whimpered. "This place feels like it wants to eat my hope... slowly... with gravy. And then burp out my skeleton as a warning."

"Keep moving," Arthur said.

They crept closer. Arthur suddenly went very still; his eyes fixed on the troll laundry flapping above the rocks.

A slow grin crept across his face.

"Kevin… do you trust me?"

Kevin blinked. "Not even slightly."

"Good. Let's do something ill-advised."

Five minutes later, they were wedged inside two of the larger trousers like particularly nervous caterpillars.

"This is the worst idea in the history of ideas," Kevin whispered. The trousers smelled like despair and wet onions. "Also, possibly feet."

Arthur shuffled them toward the pulley. "It's brilliant. We sneak in disguised as laundry, get hoisted up, and—"

"Get flattened when Wobblebottom farts mid-rescue?" Kevin hissed.

"Then keep your mouth closed."

A troll wandered past, squinting at them. Arthur went limp. Kevin tried to hum like the wind. The troll frowned, shrugged, and wandered off muttering about soup.

The pulley creaked. The line jerked. And suddenly they were rising—slowly, swaying in the wind, heading straight up the cliff face toward the fortress.

The cliffs muttered darkly: "Told you so…"

Kevin whimpered. "If I plummet to my doom inside troll pants, I'm haunting you."

"Positivity, Kevin."

Kevin squeezed his eyes shut as they ascended, flapping gently in the breeze like the world's most anxious laundry.

Above them, the fortress loomed, silhouetted against the stormy sky—black towers curling like Lardington's moustache, windows glowing an ominous gravy-orange.

Kevin groaned. "He built a castle shaped like his own facial hair."

"Of course he did," Arthur muttered. "Evil has no taste."

They rose higher, wind shrieking, trousers creaking. Wobblebottom dangled far above, being winched through towering gates, crown askew, cheeks puffing ominously.

Kevin whimpered, "If he farts and breaks the wind speed record while we're under him, I'm never speaking again."

"Excellent," Arthur said.

And with that, the two most unlikely heroes in the kingdom swayed their way up the Cliffs of Grumbles, straight toward disaster, danger, and one very bored pink hippo who was almost certainly holding back another blast.

65

The laundry pulley jolted to a stop with a metallic thunk.

Arthur and Kevin dangled for a moment in their troll-trouser disguises, gently swaying like the world's most anxious decoration. A troll wandered past muttering about soup, gave them a suspicious glance, then shrugged and scratched his armpit with a ladle.

"Move," Arthur hissed.

They wriggled out of the trousers, collapsed behind a gravy barrel, and lay gasping. Kevin clutched his chest. "I can't feel my legs. Or my dignity."

"Good," Arthur said, peering over the barrel. "You won't need either."

Kevin tried to sit up but slipped, landing in something that squelched ominously. "Please tell me that was mud," he whispered.

Arthur didn't answer.

"Of course it wasn't," Kevin muttered. "Why would it be? "Nothing's been normal since we left Wobblealot... not that Wobblealot was a shining example of sanity. They knighted a five-tonne pink hippo and nobody even questioned it.”

He pushed a glob of mud—or whatever it was—off his sleeve and looked up. The sight before him didn’t exactly restore faith in the universe.

The fortress courtyard stretched out ahead—vast, black-stoned, and trying far too hard to look important. Gargoyles shaped like ladles glared down from the walls. Gravy fountains gurgled sadly in every corner. Enormous banners hung above them, each stitched with Lardington’s face and the words *VENGEANCE IS AN ART FORM* in shiny gold thread.

Kevin’s nose wrinkled. “This place smells like gravy... and fragile masculinity.

“Accurate,” Arthur muttered.

The scrying stone buzzed. “You’ve made it inside, then,” came Twitchwhiskers’ voice, muffled slightly by chewing. “Try not to die. It would ruin my snack.”

They slipped through a side door into the fortress proper.

It was like walking through the inside of Lardington's ego. Chandeliers shaped like ladles swung overhead, dripping with suspicious gravy-coloured wax. Suits of armour stood in rows; each topped with fake moustaches. Portraits of Lardington lined the walls—twirling his moustache, standing on a pile of defeated crumpets, glaring at a mirror while the mirror glared back.

Kevin stared at one that was just Lardington reclining on a throne made of soup spoons. "Who paints this many pictures of themselves?"

"People who have therapy-resistant moustaches," Arthur muttered.

They ducked behind a decorative gravy urn as two troll guards lumbered past, arguing.

"I'm not polishing the moustache pedestal again. Last time it tried to wink at me."

"That was you in the reflection."

"Don't start."

The trolls shuffled off. Twitchwhiskers whispered from the stone, "Straight ahead, through the door marked *Absolutely Not a Secret Evil Lair*. Subtlety is not his strong suit."

The door opened into a colossal chamber—and Kevin's jaw fell open.

In the centre of the room loomed a gigantic machine shaped exactly like the Golden Gravy Boat, only fifty times larger and several hundred times more unstable. Gleaming golden panels bulged with rivets. Gravy hoses coiled like snakes across the floor, pulsing ominously. Steam hissed from vents shaped like huge moustaches. At its front, bolted on was a massive gravy cannon; an absurd, gleaming tube that looked equal parts plumbing disaster and moustache-inspired madness.

A massive scoreboard hung overhead, flashing **REVENGE POINTS: −1,003.** Underneath, someone had scrawled: *(due to bellyflop incident)*

Kevin's gaze followed the scoreboard down the curve of the machine… and froze.

"Oh no."

Arthur turned. "What?"

Kevin pointed weakly. "There's Wobblebottom."

And strapped to the nose of the golden monstrosity—mouth slightly open, crown tilted, was Sir Wobblebottom.

He was drooling gently onto the control panel, and every few seconds, he let out a quiet little fart of contentment that made a nearby spoon twitch nervously.

"Of course he's napping through his own kidnapping," Arthur muttered.

A fanfare blared from hidden trumpets.

"BEHOLD!"

A spotlight snapped on, revealing a tall, thin figure on the balcony above. His moustache gleamed like two furious commas. His suit sparkled with gravy-resistant polish.

"Lardington," Arthur growled.

"THE VERY SAME!" Lardington thundered. He spread his arms as if the whole room should gasp in awe. It didn't. A pipe just made a rude glugging noise.

"At last, the day of my GRAND GRAVY RECKONING has come!"

He jabbed a finger towards Wobblebottom. "That... that bloated pink belly flopper humiliated me! Before the whole of Grizzleham! Songs were written about it, one was called THE SPLAT HEARD 'ROUND GRIZZLEHAM!"

Kevin blinked. "Catchy."

"They made T-SHIRTS," Lardington shrieked. "And fridge magnets. Small children celebrate Bellyflop Day with custard pies! My moustache twitched for six months!"

He whirled dramatically, suit tails—fluttering. "But no longer! Tonight, I erase his legacy. My magnificent Gravy Cannon will launch him across the entire kingdom in a single glorious splat! He will crash into the sea! The splash will wipe his name from history—and coat Wobblealot in shame and delicious gravy fallout!"

He slammed a fist down on a giant red lever marked LAUNCH. A mechanical voice boomed:

"System armed. Awaiting launch sequence."

The machine rumbled to life. Gears clanked. Gravy pipes shuddered. Somewhere deep inside, something mooed.

Kevin's lips flapped soundlessly. "He's... he's going to cannonball the hippo."

Arthur's jaw tightened. "We have to stop it."

They crept along the shadowy edge of the platform. Troll technicians in lab coats bustled about, arguing over splash radius.

"More gravy pressure!"

"No, less gravy pressure!"

"It's already hissing at me!"

Twitchwhiskers' voice crackled in Arthur's ear. "You should cut the red wire." "There is no red wire," Arthur whispered.

"There's always a red wire," Twitchwhiskers said confidently. "Possibly blue."

Kevin pointed at a cluster of levers. "Maybe one of those stops it?"

"Or explodes us," Arthur muttered.

Kevin's voice climbed an octave. "Everything here smells like boiling meat sadness, Arthur. I am not emotionally equipped to touch anything."

"Do it anyway," Arthur said through clenched teeth.

Kevin inched forward, trembling. He stretched out one finger… and bumped the nearest lever.

The entire machine let out a delighted *BWOOMP,* and all the lights turned red.

An enormous screen lit up over their heads, flashing LAUNCH SEQUENCE INITIATED.

A siren wailed. Trolls shrieked and scattered. One dove headfirst into a gravy vat. Another curled up under the scoreboard and wept into his clipboard.

"Ten," boomed a mechanical voice. "Nine…"

"Undo it!" Arthur hissed.

"I DON'T KNOW HOW TO UNDO A GRAVY MACHINE!" Kevin squealed. "There's no undo button! There's just goo and misery!"

"Eight…"

Wobblebottom blinked awake. He crossed his eyes briefly, then snorted. The snort cracked a nearby window.

"Seven…"

Lardington threw back his head and laughed maniacally. "YESSS! The splat will be LEGENDARY! They will call it THE BLAST HEARD ROUND THE WORLD!"

"Six…"

Kevin clutched his hair. "We're going to die. We're going to launch a hippo and drown in hot gravy."

"Five…"

Arthur's eyes narrowed. "Right. New plan. You distract the trolls, I'll stop the machine, and Kevin—don't faint."

"Four…"

"Too late for the fainting!" Kevin wailed. "And he's about to be soup!"

Chapter 9
The Great
Escape
(with Extra Wind)
REVENGE
POINTS:
ZERO

THREE!" roared the machine.

Gravy pipes groaned. Steam hissed. The whole chamber shook with the smell of boiling onions and bad life choices.

Arthur tugged furiously at the straps, but the leather only squeaked and stretched like overcooked cheese. "Hold still!" he barked.

Kevin was flailing nearby, clutching a wrench he had no idea how to use. "This is it!

We're going to be soup! I'll be remembered as garnish! My tombstone will read:

"Here lies Kevin. He squeaked."

"Two!" shrieked the machine. Trolls panicked, slipping across the gravy-slick floor. One threw down his clipboard and yelled, "I wanted soup duty, not Armageddon duty!" before diving into a barrel.

High above, Lord Lardington spread his arms, moustache gleaming with oily righteousness. His suit sparkled under gravy-scorched torchlight.

"At last!" he cried. "The day of my revenge! The day I erase that pink menace from history!"

He jabbed a finger toward Wobblebottom, strapped to the nose of the cannon. "You think they'll remember a hippo who sat on me? No! They'll remember **me**—my vengeance, my moustache, my glory! They'll remember my name even if I have to staple it to history with gravy and spite!"

Kevin squeaked. "Stapled... with gravy?"

But Lardington was only winding up. His voice thundered over the alarms.

"They made trading cards of him! Little cardboard Wobblebottoms! Do you know how humiliating it is to lose to a flatulent pink lump who comes with shiny foil editions? They wrote songs—'The Splat Heard 'Round Grizzleham!' They sang it off-key in taverns! Children made *hand puppets!* There is a holiday named Bellyflop Day!"

He stomped his foot so hard his moustache quivered. "Well, no more! From this day forward, it is LARDINGTON they shall praise! My moustache will be carved into monuments! My villainy will echo through the ages!”

Arthur muttered, “You sound desperate.”

“Desperate?!” Lardington shrieked.
“I sound GLORIOUS!” “ONE!”
bellowed the machine.

Arthur braced. Kevin clapped both hands over his head.

And Wobblebottom... wiggled.

He had been lazily chewing through the last strap as though it were liquorice, and now, cheeks puffing like bellows, he angled his enormous pink backside with terrifying purpose.

FWWWWWWWARRRRRP.

The fart was colossal. Triumphant. Like a war trumpet played by a hippo-shaped hurricane.

The Gravy Cannon jolted backwards. Pipes screamed. Valves popped. A fountain of hot gravy shot out sideways, drenching a row of trolls who screamed, “It burns! It's seasons!”

A jet of pressurised gravy slammed into Lardington's balcony, knocking him flat on his face. "MY SUIT!" he wailed. "DRY-CLEAN ONLY!"

The machine hiccupped, belched steam, and spun its gauges so fast they flew off the dials. A red light flashed ERROR: TOO MUCH HIPPO GAS.

Arthur shouted, "Everyone down!"

Kevin wailed, "I'm already down!" and curled into a ball.

Wobblebottom let out a proud snort. Now free of the last strap, he launched himself belly-first at the control panel.

KABLOOOOOOMPF!

The bellyflop flattened the controls in one earth-shaking slap. Gears exploded. Valves burst like popcorn. A tidal wave of gravy erupted, showering chandeliers, trolls, and one unfortunate portrait of Lardington kissing his own moustache.

The scoreboard fizzed, sparked, and reset itself to:
REVENGE POINTS: ZERO.

"NOOO!" Lardington bellowed, staggering to his feet, dripping gravy. "This was my moment!"

Another fart rumbled from Wobblebottom, rattling the rafters. The remaining pipes cracked. The cannon gave a final shudder and collapsed in a glorious heap of gravy-soaked wreckage.

The chamber went silent except for the gurgle of bubbling gravy.

Trolls fled in all directions, slipping like bowling pins across the floor. One clung to the ladle chandelier, sobbing, "Tell my wife I hated soup!" before tumbling into the flood.

Arthur hauled Kevin to his feet and scowled at the triumphant, gravy-dripping hippo.

"Wonderful. We nearly died three times... for someone who clearly didn't need us." Kevin wheezed, "Next time... let's just send him a map and stay home."

Wobblebottom stood tall, dripping gravy, crown askew, cheeks puffed with pride. He let out one final, gentle toot—soft as a sigh—that toppled the last intact lever.

The wreckage gave way with a final splash, gravy cascading through the fortress.

Somewhere beneath the bubbling mess, Lardington's muffled voice gurgled: "This isn't over! My moustache... will... rise again!" followed by a wet blub.

The scrying stone at Arthur's neck buzzed. Twitchwhiskers' voice rang out, maddeningly smug. "Excellent work, gentlemen. A perfectly executed Operation Hippo Bomb Disposal. And on cue, my cheesecake has arrived. Marvelous timing all around."

Arthur groaned, flicking gravy from his beard. "Come on, Kevin. Let's get Wobblebottom home before he decides to fart the royal anthem."

Kevin whimpered. "Don't give him ideas."

But Wobblebottom simply waddled forward through the gravy flood, majestic in his own messy, gassy way. Each step left a ripple. Each ripple carried the smell of victory. And as they trudged out of the ruined fortress, a final fart echoed behind them—long, loud, and oddly triumphant. A victory fanfare, straight from the hippo himself.

Chapter 10
Home Is Where
the Hippo Is

The castle gates groaned open just as the first streaks of dawn painted the sky.

Arthur trudged through them, shoulders sagging, his clothes stiff with dried gravy. Kevin stumbled in behind him, mud-splattered, kazoo dangling from his belt like the world's least impressive sword. And waddling proudly at the rear—crown crooked, belly wobbling, cheeks puffed with pride—came Sir Wobblebottom.

The courtyard guards snapped to attention, then immediately wrinkled their noses.

One muttered, "He's back."

Another added, "And so's the smell."

Windows banged open. Word travelled faster than wildfire.

Villagers spilled into the square, rubbing sleep from their eyes. Someone unfurled a lopsided banner that read:

WELCOME BACK, WOBBLEBOTTOM
(PLEASE AIM YOUR REAR AWAY FROM THE
WINDOWS).

Another banner, clearly painted in haste, declared:

LONG LIVE THE HIPPO
(EXCEPT AT SUPPERTIME).

The crowd gagged, but cheered anyway as Wobblebottom gave them a regal snort and a fart so thunderous it rattled the shutters of the west tower.

A child pointed skyward. "It's like thunder!"

Another corrected, "Thunder doesn't smell like that."

Up on the castle balcony, Baron Twitchwhiskers appeared, cloak flapping dramatically in the breeze, monocle gleaming.

He puffed out his chest, twitched his tail, and announced, "Well, well! My daring field team returns intact. As predicted. You're welcome."

Arthur squinted up at him. "You weren't there."

"I was there in spirit," Twitchwhiskers sniffed. "And in strategy. And in snacking. Someone had to keep morale high at headquarters. Do you know how difficult it is to stir cheesecake with one paw?"

Kevin collapsed onto the cobblestones with a whimper.

"I'm never leaving the castle again. Never. Not for trolls. Not for gravy. Not even for free ice cream."

"Good," Arthur muttered. "Less chance of you getting lost in your own clothes."

Kevin groaned. "I nearly died four times."

"Three," Arthur corrected. "You tripping over your own feet doesn't count."

"I was nearly flattened by a gravy barrel!"

"Yes, that one's fair."

"And the trolls."

"Indeed."

"And the cannon."

"Technically, Wobblebottom's fault."

Kevin gave a tired laugh. "So... that one doesn't count?" Arthur sighed. "Not if Wobblebottom is involved."

The villagers swarmed closer, some clapping, some waving scraps of cloth like flags.

A baker handed Arthur a fresh loaf of bread.

An old woman pressed a jar of pickled onions into Kevin's arms, muttering, "For your nerves, dear."

And three children proudly presented Wobblebottom with a cart piled high with watermelon rinds.

The hippo's eyes lit up. He plopped down right there in the square, crown sliding over one ear, and began munching happily. Crunch. Snort. Pfffft.

The villagers cheered again, though many clutched handkerchiefs to their noses.

"He's back!" one cried.

"Just like old times!" groaned another.

Arthur leaned against the fountain, wiping a smear of dried gravy from his beard. "Well. We did it. Somehow."

"You mean he, did it?" Kevin muttered, pointing at Wobblebottom, who was now rolling onto his side to reach a particularly juicy rind.

"We nearly got turned into stew, and he belly-flopped his way out without any help from us."

Arthur's frown softened. "True. But that's Wobblebottom for you. Half chaos, half miracle, all hippo."

Twitchwhiskers preened from his balcony perch.

"And don't forget my contribution! Remote counsel, precise calculations, and an unshakable ability to nap during crises. A lesser baron would have panicked."

"No one's writing songs about your cheesecake, Twitch," Arthur called up.

"They should," Twitchwhiskers huffed. "It had a glorious crust."

Kevin sat cross-legged on the stones, arms folded tight.

"Next time you two want to chase villains, you can count me out. I'm not adventuring again. Ever. I'm going to stay inside the castle, safe and quiet. Maybe polish boots. Or clean hay. Hay doesn't explode."

Arthur gave him a sideways look. "Kevin, you'd find a way to trip over hay."

Kevin groaned. "Don't ruin this for me."

Wobblebottom crunched the last rind, gave an enormous satisfied burp, and waddled toward the castle doors. The crowd parted like a tide.

He paused halfway, turned his rear toward the courtyard, and let loose one final, rolling blast of victory that echoed through the village streets. Birds scattered. Windows rattled. A cow fainted.

The villagers stared, some in awe, some in horror. Then, slowly, applause broke out.

"Welcome home, Sir Wobblebottom!" they shouted.

Arthur pinched the bridge of his nose. "I'd forgotten how much the castle echoes."

Twitchwhiskers, still basking in his own self-importance, declared, "And thus concludes Operation Hippo Retrieval: a flawless success, punctuated by fart, fortified by cheesecake, and forever remembered as my finest hour."

Kevin groaned. "I said never again."

Arthur sighed, looking up at the sky already turning gold. "Until the next ridiculous crisis."

But for now, the castle was alive again—with laughter, banners, and the unmistakable soundtrack of a hippo chewing watermelon rinds and farting like he owned the place.

And somehow... it felt like home.

THE END.